W9-DJO-679

# RAPUNZEL

By Marianna Mayer
Illustrated by Sheilah Beckett

A GOLDEN BOOK • NEW YORK

Western Publishing Company, Inc., Racine, Wisconsin 53404

© 1991 Marianna Mayer. Illustrations © 1991 Sheilah Beckett. All rights reserved. Printed in the U.S.A. No part of this book may be reproduced or copied in any form without written permission from the publisher. All trademarks are the property of Western Publishing Company, Inc. Library of Congress Catalog Card Number: 90-84801 ISBN: 0-307-00207-1      MCMXCII

There was once a husband and wife who lived near a grand castle. The couple didn't know it, but the castle was owned by a wicked sorceress. Behind the castle wall was a wonderful garden full of beautiful flowers and good things to eat. The wife could look out and see the castle garden from her cottage.

A time came when the husband and wife were going to have their first child. The sorceress, who had no children, decided to cast a spell on the woman. If the spell worked, the sorceress could have the child for herself.

That very day the wife began to long for rapunzel, a blue-flowering plant that grew only in the sorceress's garden.

As time passed, the spell made the wife long for the plant more and more. Finally she began to feel ill and begged her husband to get some rapunzel leaves from the castle garden. She knew that if she ate a salad of the leaves, she would feel better again.

That night the husband climbed over the garden wall and stole some of the fresh green rapunzel leaves. His wife ate them greedily and began to feel better. But the taste only made her want more.

Reluctantly the husband returned night after night.
Then one evening, when the moon was full, he slipped over
the wall to find the tall, dark figure of the sorceress waiting
for him.

"Thief! How dare you steal from me?" she said angrily.

Frightened, the man fell to his knees before her and tried
to explain.

When the sorceress heard him speak of the coming of his first child, her manner changed and her voice softened.

"You may have all the rapunzel you wish, on one condition. When the child is born, you must give it to me!"

When the husband refused, the sorceress said, "I'm sure your wife will agree."

To his surprise, the man's wife did agree to give the child up, for the spell was still working. The wife said, "Surely the owner of that beautiful castle is a great lady. She will take good care of our child."

In the next few weeks the wife grew healthier. She was given all the rapunzel she wished, and rapidly her strength returned. Soon a beautiful baby girl was born to her. The baby was named Rapunzel, after the blue-flowering plant her mother loved so much.

As promised, Rapunzel's parents had to give the baby to
the sorceress. When the heartbroken parents left, the
sorceress said to herself, laughing, "Now I will have the
child all to myself!"

For twelve years she kept Rapunzel in the castle, and
the girl grew to be very beautiful. Her eyes were as blue as
the blue-flowering plant she was named after, and her long
silken hair was as golden as the sun. The sorceress never
allowed Rapunzel's hair to be cut. When it began to trail
on the floor, the sorceress made one long braid of it and
wound it around Rapunzel's head like a golden crown.

On Rapunzel's twelfth birthday the sorceress moved her to a secluded tower. The tower did not have stairs or a door, but high at the top was a small window.

When the sorceress wanted to visit Rapunzel, she stood beneath the window and called, "Rapunzel! Rapunzel! Let down your golden hair!" The girl uncoiled her long, thick braid and let it fall like a rope from the open window until it reached the sorceress's outstretched hands. The sorceress climbed to the top of the tower and entered the window.

While they were together, the sorceress combed and braided Rapunzel's hair and always asked the same question: "Who have you seen since I was last here?"

Rapunzel always answered, "No one, Stepmother." For who would the poor, lonely girl see while locked up in the tower?

One night a handsome young prince came riding
through the forest. He heard Rapunzel's sweet voice as she
sang a beautiful song. The prince followed the sound till he
came to the tower, but he could find no way in. Since it
was late, he decided to rest until morning.

At daybreak he was awakened by an old woman's harsh call. "Rapunzel!" the voice demanded. "Rapunzel! Let down your golden hair!"

All at once the golden braid came tumbling down from the open window. When the prince saw the sorceress grab hold of the braid and climb up the tower, he whispered to himself, "So that is how one is to get inside."

Patiently the prince waited, and at last he saw the sorceress leave. Then he decided to try his luck. He called, "Rapunzel! Rapunzel! Let down your golden hair." As soon as she did, he held her long braid and climbed the tower.

Rapunzel and the prince fell in love the moment they saw each other. They wanted to be together, but they had to find a way to get Rapunzel down from the tower. The prince promised to return the next day with a rope ladder. "Then you'll be free at last," he told Rapunzel.

On the following morning, when the sorceress came to visit, she asked, "Who have you seen, Rapunzel, since I was last here?"

Rapunzel couldn't tell a lie, and she told the sorceress all about the handsome prince.

The sorceress flew into a rage and took hold of Rapunzel's braid. She cut the beautiful hair with a pair of scissors—*Snip, snap! Snip, snap!*—and the braid fell to the floor. Then, in an instant, the heartless sorceress carried Rapunzel far off to the most deserted place in the whole world and left her there alone.

At nightfall, when the prince arrived to rescue
Rapunzel, he called, "Rapunzel! Rapunzel! Let down your
golden hair!" When the braid came falling down from the
window, the prince took hold of it and climbed up the
tower. But instead of seeing his beloved Rapunzel, he found
the cruel sorceress waiting for him.

She fixed her cold black eyes upon him and cast a spell
that blinded him. "Rapunzel is lost to you forever," she
cried. "You will never see her again!"

The prince fell from the window, and though he escaped with his life, he could no longer see. Lost and alone, he stumbled away to wander hopelessly in search of Rapunzel.

Years passed until at last the unhappy prince came to the most deserted place in the whole world. All of a sudden he heard a sweet voice singing. Though it had been many years since he had heard the voice, it was familiar. Eagerly he followed the sound, and soon the poor young man stood before Rapunzel.

When she saw her beloved prince, Rapunzel threw her arms around his neck and wept for joy. Her tears fell upon his eyes, and all at once the sorceress's evil spell was broken. The prince could see Rapunzel as well as ever before.

The prince led Rapunzel back to his own kingdom,
where they were welcomed with great rejoicing. At last
they were free of the wicked sorceress, and they lived out
their lives together in love.